A Locust Ate My Daddy's Underwears.

*To Aimee Jade,
Jasmine and Laura.*

**Written by: Chrissy Gillett
Illustrated by: Hazel Hewitt**

Copyright: Gillett and Hewitt, 2007
Published by Lulu.com
ISBN: 978-1-84799-261-1

OH NO!

A Locust ate my Daddy's underwears!

They were green and hanging on the line like pears.

I really hope he goes and buys more soon,

or he will be very cold in June!

A Locust ate my Daddy's underwears.

They eat everything green that they can see, if I had a green top on they would even eat me!

A locust ate my Daddy's underwears.

I really hope he goes and buys more soon, or he will be very cold in June!

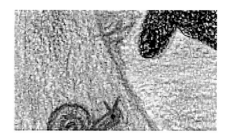

They are flying through the paddocks and eating all the trees.

My mum says don't breathe in or they will come out in your sneeze!

Now they are flying straight toward me, they want to eat my top!

They have eaten all the leaves and finished off the crop.

Then I saw a green thing hanging outside on the line.

It was drying very nicely because the day was fine.

In minutes they had come and eaten it for lunch.

Yes the locusts ate my Daddy's underwears and now they are flying while they munch!

A locust plague

"They fly, hop, travel in packs and eat everything green in their path. The Australian Plague Locust (scientific name *Chortoicetes terminfera*) is a big problem if the population gets out of control" (WA Department of Agriculture, 2006).

Locusts look the same as grasshoppers, but they are often a brown colour and that is exactly the colour they turn all green foliage into. Locusts plagues are devastating to crops, lawns, trees, plants and anything green that they come across. If there are one or two around they do not cause much damage but as they lay eggs and multiply quickly, they soon become a threat. Although they do not bite animals or humans they can be quite daunting when they take over the backyard or the school oval!

"As they multiply, they can suddenly have a 'phase change', or diapauses, which affects their shape, colour and fertility and, most problematic, they become party animals, banding together in swarms," stated the WA Department of Agriculture.

There have been huge outbreaks of locust plagues in Western Australia in 1990 and 2000 where they can cause over $20million dollars worth of damage in one season.

From April to December 2006, the Locust plagues struck again taking everything green within their path. During the drought of 2006, Australian farmers, householders, schools and shires, also lost crops and lawns to the locusts. School children ran through their ovals in a swarm of locusts.

Despite the extreme efforts of Agricultural departments, another plague is set to hatch this year.

See the Western Australian Department of Agriculture website for more information:
http://www.agric.wa.gov.au

Chrissy Gillett is a published poet, has an MA in Writing, lives on a farm in Williams WA, with her two daughters and husband and teaches Primary School Children.

Hazel Hewitt is a very talented Western Australian Artist who has her own menagerie of Australian animals in Williams, WA.
She has home-schooled 4 of her 6 children and loves her large family.

For more exciting books and news visit:
www.chrissygillett.com
and www.lulu.com